# How Billy Hippo learned his Colours

## Vivian French

### Hannah Foley

Little Billy Hippo was worried.

It was his dad's birthday and he didn't have a present for him.

"Find something pink," said his sister Betty.
"Pink is his favourite colour."

"What's pink?" asked Billy.

"Lots of things," said his brother Ben.
"Go and look."

"Flowers are pink," said Betty.
"You could find him some flowers."

Billy went to find his dad something pink.
He climbed up the river bank and walked along the path.

"Those flowers are pretty," he said.
"But I don't think they're pink."

A parrot was sitting on a branch
above his head.

"Silly Billy!" she squawked.
"Those flowers are yellow!
Yellow like the sun!"

"Bother," said Billy, and he
went on walking.

There were lots of flowers growing
in among the tall grass.
"I like those," Billy said.
"And I'm almost sure they're pink."

The parrot had followed him.

"Silly Billy!" she squawked. "Those are blue!
Blue like the sky!"
"Bother," said Billy, and he went on walking.

"I can see pink flowers!" Billy ran to pick them...

But the parrot squawked, "Silly Billy!
Those are **RED!** Red as your nose
when you've got the sneezes!"

Billy sat down.

"I'm never going to find something pink for my dad," he said,
and a tear trickled down his cheek.

The parrot flew down beside him.

"Don't cry, Billy. Look at me!
What colour are my feathers?"

Billy looked at the parrot.

"Yellow like the sun.
Blue like the sky.
Red like my nose
when I get the sneezes..."

"That's right," said the parrot.
"And I'm green like the trees.
And look at your T-shirt Billy.
That's orange, just like..."

"An orange!" said Billy.

"Exactly," said the parrot.
"But I'm not pink. Not at all."

Billy wiped away his tears. "What IS pink?"
The parrot put her head on one side.
"Have you ever seen the clouds in the early morning? Just
before the sun comes up? That's pink."

She shook her feathers. "I don't think much of pink myself,
I like red and yellow and blue and green and orange!"
And she flew away.

"Oh," said Billy, and he sighed. "I suppose I'd better go home."
Billy walked slowly back along the river bank.
He was almost home when he saw something...

**"PINK FLOWERS!"** shouted Billy,
and he picked a big bunch...

And his dad said it was his **best birthday present ever!**